TOWER HAMLETS PUBLIC LIBRARY

KT-404-334

Station

Brandon Robshaw

Published in association with
The Basic Skills Agency

Hodder & Stoughton
A MEMBER OF THE HODDER HEADLINE GROUP

TOWER HAMLETS
LIBRARIES

HEA | £3.99

1 8 MAR 2003

LOCN. | CLASS
BOWID | J ROB

ACC. No.
C1204922

Acknowledgements
Cover: Matthew Williams
Illustrations: Josephine Blake

Orders: please contact Bookpoint Ltd, 130 Milton Park, Abingdon, Oxon OX14
4SB. Telephone: (44) 01235 827720, Fax: (44) 01235 400454. Lines are open from
9.00 - 6.00, Monday to Saturday, with a 24 hour message answering service.
Email address: orders@bookpoint.co.uk

British Library Cataloguing in Publication Data
A catalogue record for this book is available from The British Library

ISBN 0 340 84848 0

First published 2002
Impression number   10 9 8 7 6 5 4 3 2 1
Year   2005 2004 2003 2002

Copyright © 2002 Brandon Robshaw

All rights reserved. No part of this publication may be reproduced or
transmitted in any form or by any means, electronic or mechanical, including
photocopying, recording, or any information storage and retrieval system,
without permission in writing from the publisher or under licence from the
Copyright Licensing Agency Limited. Further details of such licences (for
reprographic reproduction) may be obtained from the Copyright Licensing
Agency Limited, of 90 Tottenham Court Road, London W1P 9HE.

Typeset by SX Composing DTP, Rayleigh, Essex.
Printed in Great Britain for Hodder & Stoughton Educational, a division of
Hodder Headline Plc, 338 Euston Road, London NW1 3BH by Athenaeum
Press, Gateshead, Tyne & Wear.

Contents

TOWER
HAMLETS
LIBRARY

BIDDLESFORD

1

Biddlesford Station

The train was slowing down.
Ruth looked out of the window.
They were pulling into
a little country station.
The sort of country station
where no one gets on or off.
Just a bare platform
with a name plate saying BIDDLESFORD.

Tall grass and willow trees
grew behind the fence.
It was a sunny June day.
Birds were singing.

What a peaceful place, thought Ruth.
She was surprised that the station
hadn't been closed down years ago.
It looked as though it was never used.
But it was nice to stop there
for a moment's peace and quiet.

Ruth was a student.
It was the summer break
and she was going home
to stay with her parents.

She was glad the term was over.
She'd worked hard
and she needed a rest.
Besides, she had no money left.
At least she wouldn't have to
worry about money at her parents'.

Meals would be free.
No rent to pay.
Maybe she would be able to find a
summer job.
Suddenly, Ruth saw something
lying on the platform.
Something purple.
It was a twenty-pound note.

I wonder if I've got time
to jump down and get that,
thought Ruth.
If I'm quick, I should be all right.

In a moment she was out of her seat.
She opened the train door
and jumped down on to the platform.

2

The Platform

Ruth trotted across the platform.
She bent down to pick up
the twenty-pound note.
Just as her fingers were about to close on it,
something happened.
The note stirred, as if in a breeze.
Then a gust of wind must have caught it.
It was whisked away down the platform.

'Damn!' said Ruth.
She ran along the platform.

Just as she was bending down
to pick up the note, the same thing happened.
The note was whisked away from her fingers.
It ended up by the door of the ticket office,
almost as though it was trying to get away.
As though it was playing games with her.
As though it had a mind of its own.

The strange thing was,
there was almost no wind.
It was a calm, still, warm day.
Yet something must have been
moving the note.
Notes didn't move around on their own.

Quickly, she ran over to the door
of the ticket office.
As she got there,
she looked over her shoulder,
to check on the train.

Without any noise,
it was slowly pulling out of the station.

Ruth ran back to it.
She tried to pull the door open.
But now the train was moving too fast.
She couldn't get a proper grip.
The train was getting faster all the time.
She had to let go,
or she would be dragged along.

She let go and stood on the platform.
The last carriage went past her.
She watched the train get
smaller and smaller
as it went down the track.
Then it disappeared round a bend.

Ruth stood on the platform, all alone.
She couldn't believe it!
Now what was she going to do?

3

The Ticket Office

She might as well go and get
the twenty-pound note, anyway.
It had caused all the trouble,
so she might as well have it.

She walked over to the door
of the ticket office.
As she got there,
another breeze seemed to lift the note.
It was blown into the ticket office.
Ruth followed it inside.

There was no one there, and the
ticket shop window was boarded up.
'Hello?' called Ruth.
'Anyone there?'
There was no answer.

Ruth looked on the wall for a timetable.
She wanted to find out
when the next train stopped here.
But there was no timetable.
Just a few old posters on the walls.
Ruth looked again at the posters.
They were very old and faded.
One had a picture of a smiling child
drinking from a cup.
'Cocoa, two shillings a jar,' it said.
It was very strange.
The posters must have been there
for years.

It looked as though this station
was no longer used.
She would have to go into the village
and ask for help.
Find out how to get out of here.

Then she remembered
the twenty-pound note.
It was lying just by the exit.
Through the exit,
she could see cottages,
and above them trees and a blue sky.
It looked like a nice little village.

She bent to pick up the note –
and again it was whisked away.
Out through the exit it went.

Ruth followed it out into the sunlight.
Outside, she got a surprise.

4

Two Men

Two men were standing there.
It seemed as though they had
been waiting for her.
One was very fat and had a beard.
The other was tall and thin and bald.
Both men were grinning.
The tall, thin one
had only one tooth.

'Excuse me,' said Ruth.
'I've got a bit of a problem . . .'

'Yes, you have!' said the tall, thin man.

Both men laughed.
The fat man with the beard moved his hand.
Ruth saw that he was holding a string.
The string was tied
to the twenty-pound note.

The man pulled the note towards him.
He picked it up and put it in his pocket.
Then both men laughed again.
A chill ran through Ruth.

'This is the best one we've caught!'
said the fat, bearded man.

'Best ever!' said the tall, thin man.
'Nice and young. And pretty.
We'll have some fun with this one.'

'Look,' said Ruth,
'if this is some kind of joke . . .'

'But it's not a joke,'
said the fat, bearded man.
'Not a joke at all.'

They began to move towards Ruth.

5

A Race Along the Track

Ruth turned and ran.
She ran back through the gate.
Through the ticket office
and back on to the platform.

This was a mistake.
There was nowhere to go.
The two men came out
of the ticket office after her.
Ruth looked up and down the platform.
There was no exit at either end.
There was only one thing to do.
Ruth jumped down on to the track.

She ran along by the side of the rails
as fast as she could.
It wasn't easy to run.
The ground was covered with sharp stones.

After a minute or two, Ruth looked back.
The two men were coming after her.
They didn't seem to be gaining on her.
But they weren't falling behind either.
How long could she stay in front?

She was coming up to a tunnel.
It gaped before her
like a great dark mouth.
Ruth slowed down.
She didn't want to run into it.
But what else could she do?

Then she heard the sound of a train
coming down the line towards her.

6

Up the Hill

Ruth looked round wildly.
She couldn't run into the tunnel
with a train coming towards her.
If she stayed where she was
the men would catch her.
She had to get off the track.

By the side of the track was a fence
and behind that a steep, grassy bank.
Quickly, Ruth climbed over the fence.
She heard the train rush by.
She scrambled up the hill
as fast as she could.

She had to grab tufts of grass
to pull herself up.
Her heart was beating fast.

At the top of the hill, she looked back.
The two men were climbing over the fence.
The fat, bearded one
was having a bit of trouble.

There was another fence in front of her.
Ruth climbed over that too.
She pushed her way through
some bushes and ferns.

She found herself standing in a street
of pretty thatched cottages.
This must be the village of Biddlesford.
There was no one around.

Then she heard the men behind her,
crashing through the bushes.
Ruth ran down the street.

7

The Village Green

Ruth came out on to a little village green.
There was a stone church with a tower.
A little pub called The Nag's Head.
A little post office.
A duck pond
with some white ducks swimming in it.
There were some cottages
and one or two bigger houses.

There were no people to be seen.
The pub and the post office were closed.
There was no sound to be heard,
except the singing of birds.

Ruth looked around wildly.
There was no one to help her
and nowhere to hide.
Soon, the two men would be here.

Perhaps she should go and knock
at the door of one of the houses?
At that moment, she saw a woman
walking towards her.
The woman was plump and middle-aged.
She carried a basket over her arm
She looked kind and friendly.

'Hello, dear,' she said.
'Are you lost?'

'Please – you must help me!' said Ruth
'There are two men after me!
They'll be here any minute!'

'Two men?' said the woman.
'You're lucky.
Some of us can't even get one!'
She laughed.

'Please!' said Ruth
'It's not a joke!
I got off the train here by mistake.
Two men – a fat one and a thin one –
tried to trick me with a twenty-pound note.
They're after me!'

The woman stopped laughing.
'That sounds like Bill and Ben,' she said.
'Up to their old tricks again.
You poor thing.
You must have had a bad shock.
Come with me.
I live just here.'

She led Ruth up the path
to a thatched cottage.
She opened the door.
'In you go.
You'll be safe with me.'

8

Mrs Mimms' Front Room

Ruth found herself in a small front room.
There was a soft, squashy sofa.
There were easy chairs with cushions on.
There was a vase of dried flowers
on the table.
A stuffed bird in a glass case.
A clock ticked on the mantelpiece.

Ruth sat down in an easy chair.
She took deep breaths.
She could hardly believe she was safe.

'You must call the police,'
she said to the woman.
'Those men, they've got to be stopped.'

'Yes, they're naughty boys,' said the woman.
'Don't worry now, though.
You're safe here.
I'm Mrs Mimms, by the way.'

She put out her hand.
Ruth shook it.
'I'm Ruth,' she said.
'But you must call the police!'

'All in good time,' said Mrs Mimms.
'Let's have a cup of tea first.
You need one after your shock.'

She went into the kitchen.
'Biscuits, dear?' she called out.
Ruth didn't answer.

Through the window,
she had just seen the two men,
Bill and Ben.

They were walking across the green
towards the cottage.

9

Behind the Sofa

'Mrs Mimms!' Ruth called out.
'It's them!
They're coming this way!'

Mrs Mimms came out of the kitchen,
wiping her hands on a tea towel.
'All right, dear, don't you worry.
I'll sort them out.'

Through the window,
Ruth saw the two men
coming up to the garden gate.
She jumped up and hid behind the sofa.

TOWER
HAMLETS
LIBRARY

She crouched there,
her heart beating fast.

There was a knock at the door.
Ruth heard Mrs Mimms go out into the hall.
She heard the front door opening.

'Well?' said Mrs Mimms.
'What have you got to say for yourselves?'

'We got one,' Ruth heard the fat,
bearded man say.
'But she got away.'

'You silly boys!' said Mrs Mimms.
Then she laughed.
'Don't worry, lads,' she said.
'I've got her here.'